Stick & FETCH INVESTIGATE

THE WRONG END OF THE STICK

Philip Ardagh

illustrated by

Elissa Elwick

WALKER
BOOKS

Meet Sally Stick and her dog
(and best friend), Fetch.

Together, they're:
STICK & FETCH, DETECTIVES.

Like most top-notch **DETECTIVES**, Stick and Fetch are very good at working *undercover*.

Working *undercover* means pretending not to be **DETECTIVES** when they're actually detecting!

STICK & FETCH are very good at pretending to be an ordinary girl and an ordinary dog ...

... when they're really a TOP **DETECTIVE** DUO.

Fetch especially loves disguises. His
two favourites are:

1. Bunny Rabbit

2. Dog With Eye Patch

All top-notch **DETECTIVES** have an office. STICK & FETCH's detective office is Granny Stick's kitchen. (They live at Granny Stick's.) Her kitchen table is their detective desk, and that's where Sally keeps her **BIG BOOK OF DETECTIVE TALES**. It's full of very useful detective tips.

Sally carries a notebook and pencil with her at all times, along with a magnifying glass for hunting out **CLUES**. Fetch, her detective partner, is always at her side.

Fetch isn't one of those fancy breeds of dog. He's a bit of a mixture.

But he's *Sally's* dog, so as far as Fetch is concerned, that makes him the BEST kind of dog there is.

It's not every **DETECTIVE** who gets a kiss on the nose or tummy rubs from his detective partner! They're very special **DETECTIVES**.

GLASS
HALF
FULL

ne summer, Granny Stick had to go into hospital for an operation, so Sally Stick went to stay with her uncle Bob. Fetch, of course, went too.

"We stick together, don't we, Fetch?" said Sally.

WOOF! said Fetch with his mouth full.

SQUEAK!

Sally rubbed Fetch between the ears, just the way he likes. "We'll have to do our **DETECTING** out of a temporary **headquarters**," she said.

Sally Stick's uncle Bob is an artist. He paints such great, big paintings that people need great, big walls to hang them on. He lives on his own in a house crammed top to bottom with books and stuff. ("Stuff" is what Uncle Bob himself calls it.) *Stuff* includes:

- ★ empty biscuit tins
- ✿ odd shoes
- ★ broken clocks
- ✳ glass paperweights, and
- ✿ lots and lots and LOTS
     of biscuit crumbs!

BISCUITS

BOING!

At the back of the house is Uncle Bob's studio, where he paints all day. It's a large room with lots of windows and a glass roof. The rest of the house smells of dust and engine oil and old books and biscuits, but the studio is a lot tidier and simply smells of paint.

"You are both welcome to go into any room in the house," said Uncle Bob, the day **STICK & FETCH** arrived, "except my studio. That is the only rule."

Later, Sally was sitting at the kitchen table with her uncle. It was much bigger than Granny's table. And round. Sally was drinking a glass of milk while her uncle was enjoying a glass of juice.

WOOF! said Fetch. He was drinking water from a bowl in the corner. Sally had put his bed there, too. She had chosen a nice, cosy spot for it – though they both knew that, more likely than not, he'd end up sleeping on *her* bed.

In Fetch's bed was his favourite toy, Squeaky the duck, and on the table was Sally's **BIG BOOK OF DETECTIVE TALES**. There had been NO WAY they were leaving either of *those* at home.

"Mum tells me you're **DETECTIVES**," said Uncle Bob, through a mouthful of biscuit.

It was funny for Sally to think of Granny Stick as Uncle Bob's mum!

"Yes," she said. "We're STICK & FETCH, DETECTIVES."

"We've solved a lot of cases," added Fetch.

"Fetch says that we've solved a lot of cases," said Sally, because all her uncle could hear was **WOOF! WOOF! WOOF!** (That's all that *anyone* but Sally hears when Fetch is talking.)

"Well, while you're here, perhaps you could solve the case of my missing glasses," said Uncle Bob, putting down his glass of juice. "There's a reward."

"A reward?" barked Fetch. He wagged his tail. Dogs often wag their tails when they're excited. And to **STICK & FETCH** there's nothing more exciting than a case! "What kind of reward?"

"Fetch was wondering—" began Sally.

"What the reward might be?" Uncle Bob suggested.

"Yes!" said Stick and Fetch, together.

WOOF!

Uncle Bob paused. To be honest, he hadn't thought that far ahead. Then he had an idea. "Sausages," he said. "The reward will be lots and lots of sausages!"

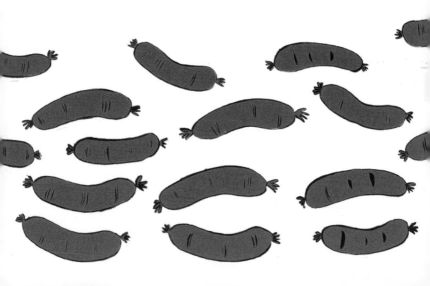

Fetch banged his wagging tail on
the floor in doggy delight. Like most dogs,
Fetch LOVES sausages.

Sally pulled her **DETECTIVE** notebook
and **DETECTIVE** pen out of the **DETECTIVE**
pocket on the front of her dress.

"What do the missing glasses look like?" she asked. She had a milk moustache from her own glass on her top lip.

"Round, like most glasses," said her uncle, staring thoughtfully at the rim of his glass of juice. "With gold rims. Would you like another biscuit?" He picked up a tin with a picture of a big, smiling cat on the lid. Luckily, Fetch couldn't see it from the floor. Fetch does NOT like cats.

"No time for biscuits!" declared Sally Stick. She'd been busy writing down what Uncle Bob had said. "We have **DETECTING** to do! You get back to your painting and we'll have this case solved by suppertime, Uncle Bob!" She gulped down the last of her milk, got up and put the glass by the sink.

THE CASE OF THE
MISSING GLASSES

Round

Gold rims

Another ~~biscuit?~~

Fetch bounded over to her side. "Ask your uncle when he last saw the glasses," Fetch suggested.

"Good idea, partner!" said Sally.

"All I know is that they're in the house somewhere!" Uncle Bob sighed when Sally asked him.

✢

Sally thought it would be a good idea to draw a REWARD POSTER. Wasn't that what *DETECTIVES* did when they wanted to find something? She found some writing paper and crayons in a drawer in the kitchen and set to work.

REWARD

Anyone who can give

infurmation about

famous artist Bob Stick's

missing glasses

with gold rims

shood contact

STICK & FETCH
DETECTIVES

There is a REWARD!

"That's VERY good," said Fetch. He was very proud of Sally. Then a worried look came over his face. "If someone sees the poster and finds Uncle Bob's glasses, will they get all the reward? Will they get ALL the sausages?"

"No, silly," said Sally. "If that happens, you and I will share the reward with them. We did the poster after all."

Fetch added a paw print at the bottom of the poster just to show he'd played his part.

They pinned the poster to the front gate, then began the search.

"We'll start in the kitchen," said Sally. "That's usually where people keep cups and mugs and glasses."

"We forgot to ask what kind of glasses!" woofed Fetch. At home, Granny Stick had LOTS of glasses. There were:

🍸 glasses with stems

☕ glasses with handles

🥣 special glasses with gold spots, and

🍹📦📦📦📦📦📦 lots of different glasses for juice and water and 𝐹𝐼𝒵𝒵𝒴 𝒟𝑅𝐼𝒩𝒦𝒮.

"That doesn't matter, partner," said Sally. "Uncle Bob won't have many glasses with gold rims. They must be for EXTRA SPECIAL drinks. We'll know them when we find them."

They did find lots of glasses, not just in the kitchen but dotted about the house.

❋ One had been used as a vase
and had dead flowers in it.

❋ One had a paintbrush in it,
along with some dirty water.

❋ Four had various levels of water
in them.

❋ One, on a windowsill, was SO old
and dusty it looked like frosted glass
when it was actually clear.

And that wasn't counting the one in Uncle Bob's bathroom with his toothbrush and toothpaste tube in it. Nor the clean ones in the cupboard.

Not a single glass had a gold rim.

"This is going to be harder than I thought," said Sally. She plonked herself down in an old wooden swivel chair in Uncle Bob's very cluttered study and rested her elbows on top of the very cluttered table he used as his desk. "I need a rest," she said.

"Me too," barked Fetch, jumping up onto his **DETECTIVE** partner's lap. There was a small machine on the table. Fetch gave it a good sniff to see if that would tell him what it was. Like most things in Uncle Bob's house, it smelled of dust and oil and biscuits. He gave up.

"Do you know what this is?" asked Sally. "It's called a typewriter. It's what people used to write with before computers."

Fetch peered at it. "Where's the screen?"

"There isn't one," Sally explained. "The words print straight onto the paper.

It's a sort of old-fashioned instant-printing computer." Granny Stick had told her all about them.

Sally went and fetched another piece of paper from the kitchen drawer and tried to work out how to feed it into the typewriter. She got there in the end. "Brilliant!" she said. "Now we can type up the **DETECTIVE** report for The Case of the Missing Glasses."

34

The big difference between an old typewriter and a modern-day computer, Sally Stick discovered, is that you can't undo mistakes on a typewriter. You have to do lots of crossings-out and corrections afterwards.

She had quite a few goes and used quite a few pieces of paper before she ended up with a report that she and Fetch were happy with.

```
STTICK AnD FETCH Detectves CASE -
Bob sticks MISING GLASSSES REPORT
- wE searched the house from
topto bottom and found lotts of
glasses. None of THEM HAD gold
rims. We have putup dwanted
pozter. NEXT REPRT Tommorow.
```

Fetch thought it looked VERY professional.

"Let's give this to our *CLIENT*," said Sally.

"Who?" Fetch barked.

"Uncle Bob, of course," said Sally.

"Of course!" woofed Fetch.

Sally knocked on the door of Uncle Bob's studio.

"Coming!" he said, and opened it. "Did you find them?" he asked.

Sally thrust the report into his hand. To read it, Uncle Bob took off the spectacles resting on top of his head.

Uncle Bob looked at the pair of glasses in his hand and at Stick and Fetch, then at the glasses again: the round, gold-rimmed glasses...

His mouth fell open. His eyes widened. "That's amazing!" he said. "That's incredible. You've found my glasses!"

"We have?" asked Fetch. ***WOOF?***

"We have," said Sally with a nod. "So this will need updating!" She took the report from her uncle's hand.

"You really are an excellent pair of ***DETECTIVES***, aren't you?" said Uncle Bob. He was clearly impressed.

*

"But we *didn't* find his glasses!" woofed a very puzzled doggy ***DETECTIVE***, sitting on the sofa later.

"We must have," said Sally. "The ***CLIENT*** is always right. We must be such good ***DETECTIVES*** that we sometimes solve cases without even realizing it."

But Fetch had stopped listening. He
was distracted. He could smell something.
Something stronger than the dust and
the oil and the biscuits. He could smell
cooking. He could smell SAUSAGES.

A BIT
OF
BEAVER
BOTHER

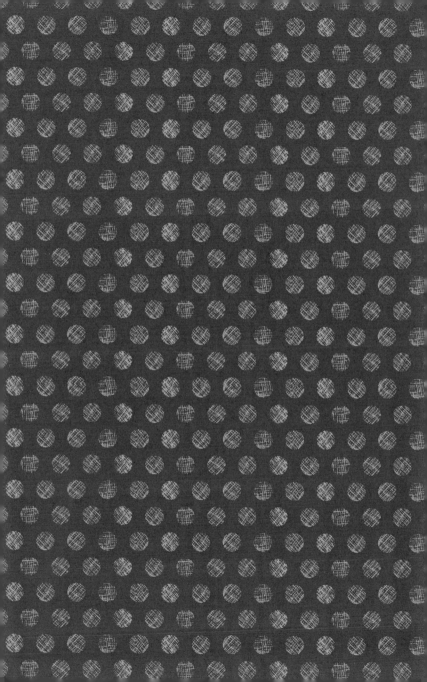

A few days after Sally and Fetch arrived at Uncle Bob's, he needed to go into town to buy art supplies. Stick and Fetch went with him in his battered old van.

Uncle Bob dropped them off at the library and gave Sally his library card so she could take out some books. Sally loves books, especially reading them to Fetch. (He likes most books, as long as they don't have cats in them.)

"I'll see you on the green by the clock tower at one o'clock," said Uncle Bob. "Then we can go and choose a *Get Well Soon* present for Granny, to go with the card you made her."

"She will get well soon, won't she?" Fetch asked Sally a little anxiously.

"Of course she will!" said Sally and patted him on the nose.

In the library, Sally Stick found a book
of animals and started flipping through it.
There was a big photograph of a beaver
inside. "They build dams," she told Fetch.

"What's a dam?" asked Fetch. *WOOF?*
WOOF?

"It's a barrier across a river or stream,"
Sally explained. "Beavers build them from
trees that they've chopped down."

46

"Beavers are very good at chopping down trees. They use their teeth."

"Wow!" said Fetch, studying the picture. It showed a H-U-G-E tree gnawed in two!

Next, Sally turned to the section on lions and tigers. Fetch doesn't like lions and tigers because they're just big cats. Back home, Fetch's arch-nemesis is a cat called Tofu. Fetch certainly wasn't missing Tofu while they were staying with Uncle Bob!

 Time always whizzes by when Stick and Fetch look at books together, so it was lucky that Sally caught sight of the library clock when she did.

"We'd better get going!" she said. "We're supposed to meet up with Uncle Bob soon!"

They thanked the nice librarian lady, who had been happy to let Fetch in despite the fact that dogs aren't really allowed in the library.

They started to walk down the hill towards the green.

"Look!" Fetch gasped.

Up ahead was a lamp post broken in two. There was a little stump at the bottom, and the rest of it lay on its side. It looked *just* like one of the chopped-down trees in the library book.

"BEAVERS!" said Sally and Fetch at exactly the same time.

They were both wondering what beavers were doing chopping down – *chomping* down – lamp posts around the town. It wasn't as if there was a river to build a dam in!

Fetch looked at the broken lamp post. He gave it a sniff to see if he could pick up any beaver-scent. Mind you, he didn't have the slightest idea what a beaver should smell like. And even if he had, his nose didn't seem to be working properly. It was as if it was full of biscuit crumbs.

"Sniffed anything interesting?" asked Sally. She pulled Granny Stick's old magnifying glass from her dress pocket and started peering at the pavement around the lamp post.

"All I can smell is biscuity exhaust fumes and biscuity baked beans," Fetch admitted.

"BEANS?" said Sally, standing straight.

"Yes," said her furry friend. "Baked beans!"

There were four or five baked bean tins on the pavement near the fallen lamp post. A couple of them were squashed open with beans and tomato sauce spilling onto the pavement.

"Of course!" said Sally Stick, studying the tins through the magnifying glass. (All that did was make the writing on the labels look bigger.) "I'm trying to remember what it said in the animal book... It said that beavers eat *bark*—"

Fetch barked.

"—and leaves and shrubs and ferns and corn and ... BEANS!"

"Wow!" said Fetch.

"If we'd found just one of these, there would be room for doubt, Fetch," said Sally. "But put both **CLUES** together and it can only mean one thing. There's a beaver on the loose!"

Stick and Fetch both looked around to see if there was any sign of one.

Fetch was distracted by a pigeon showing an interest in the spilled beans. It was giving him a funny look, so he tried to outstare it.

"But where will it build its dam if there isn't a river or lake near by?" said Sally. She shooed away the pigeon to "preserve the CRIME SCENE". (Her **BIG BOOK OF DETECTIVE TALES** had a lot to say about preserving a **CRIME SCENE**, so it must be important.)

Sally looked around for more **CLUES**. Her eyes came to rest on a large building with a great big wave painted on it. On the front of the building was a sign with two words written in large blue letters:

"There!" Sally pointed. "Maybe the beaver is planning to dam that swimming pool!"

"That could cause a flood!" said Fetch, horrified. He added a growl to show that he was NOT happy. He was imagining

whole families being swept out of the pool and down the road on a huge wave.

The **DETECTIVE** duo hurried over. There was a **NO DOGS** sign outside.

Fetch thought it was silly having a notice because not all dogs can read. Sally Stick thought it was silly because she and Fetch were working on an important case and she needed her **DETECTIVE** partner by her side.

The pair were standing outside wondering what to do when a woman walked by pulling a big box on a trolley. Sitting on the top of the box was a large teddy wearing armbands.

Before Fetch knew quite what was happening, Sally had picked him up and plonked him on top of the box by the bear.

"Sit very still," she hissed. "Pretend to be stuffed!"

Fetch tingled with excitement. Pretending to be a teddy meant that he was pretending to be something that he wasn't. It meant pretending NOT to be a **DETECTIVE**, which meant that he was working *undercover*!

He felt a *very* important dog.

Blissfully unaware that she had an extra passenger, the woman pulling the trolley walked through the entrance, the automatic doors SWOOSHING aside for her, and raised her hand in greeting to a bald man working at the reception desk. He smiled and waved her through.

Sally Stick wandered into the foyer after them, making sure that her **DETECTIVE** notebook, pencil and magnifying glass were out of sight.

Sally didn't want to
cause panic about a beaver attack, so she
was working *undercover* too. She was
pretending to be an *ordinary girl*.

"Hello," she said to the man on reception.

"Hello," said the man. His thick glasses
reminded Sally of swimming goggles.

The woman with the trolley, meanwhile, disappeared around the corner and pushed open a pair of swing-doors and marched through. Fetch jumped off the trolley before it disappeared after her. Stick caught up with him.

"Good work, **DETECTIVE**," she said,
giving him a pat.

Fetch looked around the foyer out
of sight of the reception desk. Its highly
polished blue lino floor and pale blue
walls gave the place a watery feel.

So did the smell of chlorine coming from the swimming pool.

Fetch wondered how on EARTH a beaver could have got in undetected. He asked Sally.

"Good question, **DETECTIVE**!" said Sally. "There aren't any NO BEAVERS signs, but that's probably because there aren't *usually* any beavers around. Perhaps it found a back way in. Let's go!"

Just then, the double swing-doors swung open the other way and out walked a ... a ...

"A GIANT BEAVER!" cried a stunned Sally Stick.

It *was* giant. It was as tall as the woman. And its goofy grin revealed two huge front teeth.

Perfect for gnawing down lamp posts, thought Fetch.

The beaver walked straight past them, its huge flat beaver tail dragging along behind it. It wore a cap with LITTLE BEAVERS written on it.

68

"It's trying to blend in," Stick whispered. "The cheek of it!"

It wasn't a very **DETECTIVEY** thing to do but Fetch sunk his dog teeth into the passing tail and held on tight. The giant beaver didn't so much as flinch. It was as though it didn't feel a thing!

69

Now Fetch found himself being pulled along behind the beaver on the slippery blue leisure-centre floor.

Stick was speechless!

Before Fetch knew what was happening, the beaver had pushed open *another* set of swing-doors, this time leading to the swimming pool, and was striding through them.

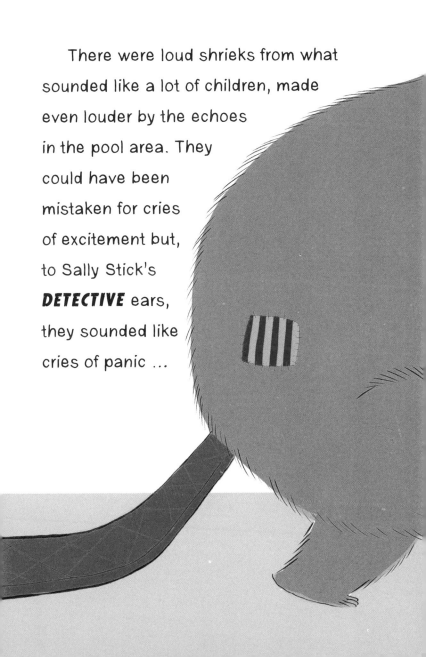

There were loud shrieks from what sounded like a lot of children, made even louder by the echoes in the pool area. They could have been mistaken for cries of excitement but, to Sally Stick's **DETECTIVE** ears, they sounded like cries of panic ...

... panic from a group of children who had just come face-to-face with a beaver about to dam their swimming pool!

Slipping in behind her **_DETECTIVE_**
dog partner, who had now wisely let go
of the beaver's tail, Sally could see that
everything had been set up for some sort
of poolside prize-giving.

"That beaver's going to ruin it for everyone!" said Fetch. His bark echoed around the swimming pool. WOOF! WOOF! WOOF! Woof! Woof! Woof! —oof! —oof! —oof!

All eyes turned to **STICK & FETCH**, standing alone by the entrance.

Everyone's eyes, including the beaver's.

Uh-oh! They would have to act NOW...

"That showed HIM!" said Sally with glee
as she ran from the building, a dripping
wet Fetch close behind.

WOOF, said Fetch, panting. It would, indeed, be a very unwise beaver who risked trying to dam a swimming pool on STICK & FETCH's patch again.

Flushed with success, the **DETECTIVE** duo bounded down the hill and reached the green just as the clock struck one o'clock. Two minutes later, Uncle Bob appeared, carrying a bag in each hand. One was full of brushes, paints and other art supplies.

The other appeared to be full of pouches.

"Sorry I'm a few minutes late," said Uncle Bob. He didn't seem to notice that his niece's dog was soaking wet. Or if he did, he didn't think it was important. (Artistic types can be like that.) "There was a bit of excitement at the shop. Their delivery van had an accident earlier. The driver skidded to avoid a cat and hit a lamp post."

"A bad day to be a lamp post," said Sally Stick. "Another one got chomped down by a beaver earlier."

"Really?" said Uncle Bob, but his mind was elsewhere.

"Really," said Fetch. But, of course, all Uncle Bob heard was ...

OUT OF THE BAG

Granny Stick was still in hospital. She'd had her operation and was feeling a lot better but, according to Uncle Bob, she was *recuperating*.

"What does that mean?" Sally asked.

"It means she needs to stay in hospital a little longer to get better," Uncle Bob explained. "You can talk to her on the phone this evening."

Fetch was very excited when Sally told him that Granny was on the mend.

"You can bark down the phone to her this evening," said Sally. "She'll like that."

They had made their own **DETECTIVE** office at Uncle Bob's. Sally had given the table in the study a good clean. Fetch, meanwhile, had sniffed out a metal desk calendar. They had also added some important-looking books, and Sally had placed her ***BIG BOOK OF DETECTIVE TALES*** on top of the pile. She had even made a STICK & FETCH desk sign. Everything looked very official.

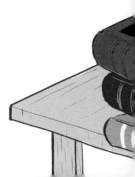

They even had an old radio that still worked. Sally was twiddling the dial when the local news came on:

There has been a spate of bag-snatching in Meanwhile Park. Members of the public are advised to be extra vigilant and hold on tight to their belongings.

"What does **spate** mean?" asked Fetch.

"I've no idea," admitted Stick.

"What about **vigilant**?"

"That means being on your guard," said Sally. "Being extra careful."

Fetch is very proud of Sally Stick because she knows the meaning of lots of big words — and **vigilant** is much bigger than **spate**.

But they BOTH knew what bag-snatching was.

"Perhaps we could give the police a helping hand?" said Sally. "It would be useful for them to have two experienced **DETECTIVES** helping them out."

WOOF! said Fetch. "Good idea!"

"Let's ask Uncle Bob if we can all go to Meanwhile Park this afternoon," Sally suggested.

This is how she and Fetch came to be on a playground roundabout later that day, spinning round and about. Uncle Bob settled on a bench over by the bandstand and read an art magazine.

The pair may have looked like a typical girl out with her dog, but this couldn't

have been further from the truth. STICK &
FETCH were *DETECTIVES* on a case and
on a roundabout. That way they could
keep an eye out in all directions for the
bag-snatcher.

"I'm getting a bit dizzy," admitted Fetch, after a while.

"Then let's split up," said Stick. "You keep a lookout by that bench while you get over your dizzification—"

"Is that a word?" asked Fetch, greatly relieved.

"I think so," said Sally. (It isn't.) "I'll go over by those trees and watch from there."

"We need a signal," said Fetch. "In case we spot anything."

"Just bark," said Sally.

Fetch wagged his tail. He had never heard Sally bark before. He was sure she would be very good at it, and told her so.

Sally laughed. "Not *me*, silly. *You* bark! I'll simply go, *Here, boy!* As though I'm calling you."

"Good plan, Stick," said Fetch. **WOOF!**

"Thank you, Fetch," said Stick. "Keep your eyes peeled."

So Fetch bounded over to an empty bench and sat under it, while Sally wandered over to a clump of trees, trying to look like an ordinary, everyday girl wandering over to a clump of trees because that's what you did in a park. She was very good at it.

Fetch didn't feel quite so dizzy now. He was ready to resume duties when he heard a **RIBBET!**

He was not alone! A frog had also decided to sit under the bench. Fetch was tempted to shoo it away, but he decided to try to outstare it instead. This seemed to work until, with one lazy leap,

the frog landed on his nose. Fetch stood up in shock and banged his head on the underside of the bench.

Ouch!

At least the jolt made the frog hop off and away. The cheeky thing!

Fetch settled back down again. He watched a girl on a skateboard whizz

past, a little boy drop the scoop of ice cream from his cone and burst into tears – Fetch would go along and lick that up later

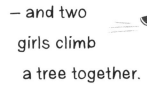

– and two girls climb a tree together.

Then a man came and sat himself on the bench, his legs blocking Fetch's view. Suddenly, Fetch switched back into **DETECTIVE** mode.

He sniffed the man's ankles. The man was wearing grubby white trainers and light blue socks and jeans, with a flash of hairy leg between the top of the socks and the bottom of his jeans. He smelled of biscuit kebabs. Fetch sniffed again: *doner* kebabs. The ones you get in pitta bread.

Fetch looked through the slats of the bench at the man above. He had dark hair spiked up at the front with gel and was wearing a baggy jacket over a T-shirt with a bulldog on it. Fetch wagged his tail. If the man had been wearing a *cat* T-shirt that would *not* have been good. He thought of his arch-nemesis Tofu and gave a shivery doggy shudder. How could *anyone* like cats?

The man had a black leather bag on his lap and was rummaging through it.

You'd better be careful with that, thought Fetch. *There's been a **spate** of bag-snatching in the park and you need to be extra **vigilant**. You're lucky* STICK & FETCH *are here to protect you.*

The man pulled out a purse, then quickly stuffed the bag under the bench, narrowly missing the *undercover* dog underneath! Then, to Fetch's surprise, the man stood up and started walking away, slipping the purse into his pocket.

He's forgotten his bag! thought Fetch.

Fetch didn't want to bark because they were on a case and Stick might think it was a signal that he'd spotted the bag-snatcher. Instead, he picked up the bag in his mouth and chased after the man,

dragging the bag along the path with him. He passed the skateboarder and a workman in overalls painting a fence.

The man from the bench heard the kerfuffle, turned round and saw that ... the bag was following him!!!

"Go away!" he said, shooing Fetch with his hands. But he wasn't looking where he was going, and he ran SMACK into Sally, who'd just appeared from the clump

of trees. Sally went flying, the man went flying ... and so did five or six wallets and purses from his pockets before he hit the ground!

"That's him!" shouted an old lady, charging across the grass. "That's the man who stole my bag! And there it is," she said, pointing at the bag still in Fetch's mouth. "Good doggy!"

Fetch let go of the bag. "*Doggy?*" he said. "Madam, I am Fetch of STICK & FETCH, DETECTIVES."

A ring of people had begun to form around them. Uncle Bob appeared, magazine in hand. "Are you OK, Sally?" he asked.

Just then, a policeman, who'd been following the old lady, arrived on the scene. He was a bit out of shape.

(Nowadays he spends rather more time giving crime-prevention talks and drinking tea than chasing criminals.)

He looked at Stick. And he looked at Fetch. And he was about to help the man

in the bulldog T-shirt up and to apologize and explain that the girl and her dog probably meant no harm … when he saw the bag and the wallets and purses scattered across the grass.

So he arrested him instead.

Everyone clapped.

"It's thanks to this girl and her dog," said the fence-painter. "I saw it all."

"This is my niece Sally and her dog Fetch," said Uncle Bob proudly, putting his arm around Sally's shoulders. "They're **DETECTIVES**."

Now *everyone* wanted to pat and

praise Fetch, but he managed to push his way over to Sally.

"Good work, Stick," he said. **WOOF! WOOF!**

"Good work, Fetch," said Stick.

That evening, they had LOTS to tell
Granny Stick on the phone. Although she
was in hospital, she sounded just like
ordinary Granny and that made Sally happy.

"It sounds to me like you're having fun at Uncle Bob's," said Granny Stick.

"Uncle Bob is very nice," said Sally, "but we do miss you."

"Is he feeding you all right?" Granny asked.

"Yes," said Sally. What she *didn't* tell her was that they mainly ate sausages ... and biscuits.

"What an exciting day," said Sally in bed that night, Fetch curled up at her feet.

WOOF! said Fetch. "I love being a **DETECTIVE**."

"And I love being a **DETECTIVE** with you," said Sally. With that, she rubbed her partner between the ears and kissed him goodnight.

BED
TIME

etch was standing at the patio doors leading out from Uncle Bob's kitchen to his back garden. The garden was much, much bigger than Granny Stick's and much more overgrown.

Suddenly, Fetch growled and started pawing the glass.

"Why are you growling?" asked Sally Stick. Fetch isn't really a growly kind of dog. "No! Wait! Don't tell me. Let me put my **DETECTIVE** skills to the test. You've spotted a cat!"

WOOF!
said Fetch.

Sally was busy sticking things into a scrapbook. "It's crazy how cats are allowed to go anywhere they like," she said. "If you decided to wander around other people's back gardens, you'd get into trouble. But cats get away with it." She was rubbing a glue stick on the back of a newspaper cutting. "And you don't exactly see many **NO CATS** signs, do you?" She picked a crumb of Maryland Cookie off the back of the clipping.

"Probably because cats are too stupid to read," said Fetch. That made him feel a LOT better. He padded over to his **DETECTIVE** partner.

"I'm doing **paperwork**," Sally explained.

Fetch nodded his doggy head wisely.

"There's a lot of **paperwork** involved in being half of a top **_DETECTIVE_** duo," he agreed.

"Don't I know it!" said Sally. "This is the latest newspaper article about us, so I'm putting it on file." She held up the scrapbook to show him. (She'd made sure she brought it with her to Uncle Bob's.)

The truth be told, the catching-the-bag-snatcher article is

GIRL AND DOG CATCH BAG THIEF!

the *only* newspaper article about STICK &
FETCH solving a *CRIME*. So far. That's not
the only time they've been in the paper,
though. When they were much younger
— and smaller — they were runners-up in
the Baby and Pet Competition AND the
Toddler and Pet Competition!

Sally Stick put the lid on her glue
stick and began flipping back through the
scrapbook. She found the picture of her
as the (second) cutest baby and Fetch
as the (second) cutest pet, and the

one of them as the (second) cutest toddler
and (second) cutest, slightly larger, pet...

There was a tap at the patio doors.
Fetch leapt all feet off the floor in surprise.

A girl was standing there. She was tall
and thin, with long hair. "Hello!" she said
through the glass. "I've got a message for
Mr Stick."

For a moment, Sally Stick wondered who Mr Stick was. Then she remembered that Uncle Bob was Bob Stick.

"He's in his studio at the moment," she said importantly. "He's not to be disturbed."

"Can you give him the message then, please?" said the girl.

"Just a minute," said Sally. She got out her **DETECTIVE** notebook and pencil. "Let me start by taking your name."

"My name?"

"Yes."

"It's Jemma."

Sally Stick wrote down: JEMMA.

"Age?"

"Sorry?"

"Don't apologize," said Sally.

She's very good at this, thought Fetch.

"Er... Thirteen."

Fetch growled. A cat — a great, big, fat, ginger-and-white one — was now rubbing around Jemma's legs, and *Jemma didn't seem to mind.* This was **OUTRAGEOUS**!!!

"OK, Jemma," said Sally. "What's the message for my uncle Bob?" She had her stubby pencil poised above the notebook, ready to write it down word for word.

"To warn Mr Stick that Tommy will be around this afternoon to dig the beds," said Jemma.

Sally was about to ask her more when the girl dashed off. That was probably because Fetch could no longer bear the sight of the cat being all friendly and had slavered all over the window. And dog dribble is NOT a pretty sight.

"Warn Uncle Bob that Tommy is going to dig the beds?" said Sally. "This sounds serious..."

"Should we tell Uncle Bob?" Fetch barked.

"When he's painting, he doesn't like to be disturbed, except in emergencies," Sally reminded him.

"This sounds like an emergency to

me," said Fetch. He didn't like the idea of someone going digging in someone's bed. They might damage the mattress or the pillow ... or even a favourite squeaky toy!

"You're forgetting who we are," said Sally. "We're STICK & FETCH, DETECTIVES.

We've been given a warning so we can put a stop to it. Let's make sure no one digs in our beds!"

*

Stick and Fetch went to Uncle Bob's study, their temporary office. This was the place to talk ***DETECTIVE***-talk.

"What do people normally dig for?" asked Sally, notebook in hand.

"That's easy," woofed Fetch. "Bones, or ... treasure ... buried treasure!"

"Of course!" said Sally. "And Uncle Bob's house is FULL of all sorts of amazing things. Maybe there's something valuable hidden in one of the beds!"

"But wouldn't you need a spade to dig for something hidden in a bed?" asked Fetch.

"Well," said Sally, "the other week, Granny was looking for her hospital appointment letter. She said that she was

going to DIG it out of the sideboard drawer, but she just used her hands. Maybe Jemma meant that this crook Tommy is going to search our beds for buried treasure with his hands."

Fetch growled again. Even the name *Tommy* sounded like the name of a villain to him.

They searched Fetch's bed first – the
one they'd brought from Granny Stick's
– because it was the nearest, as well
as being the smallest and the easiest to
search. (It is a dog basket with its very
own bone-patterned blanket. Sally saved
up to buy Fetch the blanket with her pocket
money, so Fetch loves it all the more.)

"No buried treasure here," said Sally.

Fetch was not so sure, and he reminded Sally that Squeaky was very valuable.

"Yes, he is," said Sally. "But I don't think he'll be what Tommy is after."

SQUEAK!

Next, they searched Sally's bed.
Somehow Fetch got between the duvet
and the white duvet cover. He pretended
to be a polar bear and then a ghost dog.

WOOOOOOOH!

Then they remembered that they were supposed to be doing some serious investigating.

There were a lot of rooms in Uncle Bob's house, most of them full of junk. But some of them also contained beds.

In one bed alone they found:

* a brass door handle
* a HUGE wooden pepper-grinder that looked like a giant chess piece
* a papier-mâché boot

Soon, the only bed they hadn't searched was Uncle Bob's. Stick and Fetch stood outside his bedroom door. "He did say we could go anywhere except the studio," said Sally. "And this is **DETECTIVE** business. Whatever this crook Tommy is after *must* be in here."

"I wonder how this villain, Tommy,

plans to get into the house," said Fetch.

"Who knows how master criminals operate?" said Sally with a shrug.

They were very careful when they searched Uncle Bob's bed. They only knocked over the jug of water on his bedside table, not his glass, and only one slipper ended up inside his pillowcase.

It was Fetch who was the first to find something, when he was sniffing under the mattress. He grabbed hold of whatever it was and pulled it out with his teeth.

"Uncle Bob's wallet!" said Sally with excitement. "So THAT'S what this Tommy **CROOK** is after: Uncle Bob's money! And now he'll go away empty-handed and defeated!"

They hurried back downstairs to tell Uncle Bob. They could hear voices. Sally's uncle had come out of his studio and gone into the garden to talk to a skinny young man who'd come to do some gardening.

"You could have let me know you'd be coming today, Tommy," said Uncle Bob. "I'd have bought extra biscuits!" He offered the young man a Bourbon.

"Thank you, Mr Stick," said Tommy,
taking one. "I did ask my sister to let you
know."

Sally and Fetch bounded outside.

Tommy patted Fetch. "Such a
handsome dog!" he said.

Fetch banged his tail on the ground
in delight.

"Oh, you found my wallet!" exclaimed Uncle Bob when he saw what Sally was holding. "I'm always hiding it and then forgetting where!"

"All in a day's work for STICK & FETCH," said Sally modestly.

"Well, you ARE good **DETECTIVES**," said Uncle Bob.

"We're just doing our job, sir," said Fetch. Although, of course, all Uncle Bob and Tommy could hear was **WOOF! WOOF!**

But his **DETECTIVE** partner, the Stick from STICK & FETCH, understood every single word.

HOME AGAIN

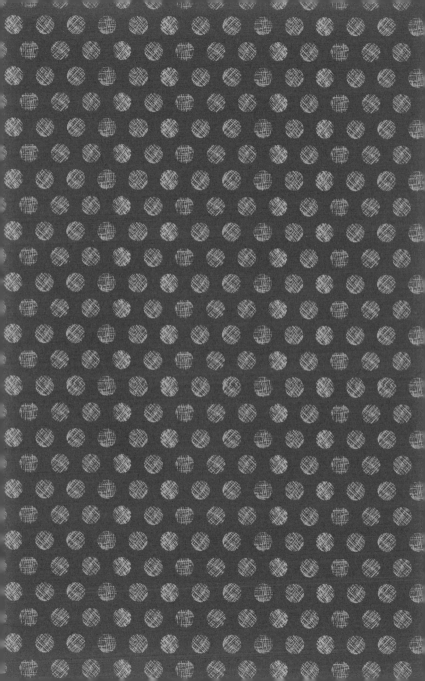

"I'm so glad you got on well with your Uncle Bob," said Granny Stick. She was now back from hospital, fully recovered, and Stick and Fetch were back home with her. "I knew you would."

"Yes," said Sally.

WOOF! said Fetch, who was very pleased to be reunited with one of his favourite rubber bones.

"And Fetch didn't mind Nipper?" asked Granny.

CHEW!
CHEW!

CHEW!

"Nipper?" asked Sally.

WOOF?

"Bob's cat, silly!" said Granny.

The rubber bone fell from Fetch's mouth with a squeak.

Cat?!

SQUEAK!

"Uncle Bob has a cat?" said Sally. "That's impossible. Fetch would have sniffed it out with his doggy **DETECTIVE** nose!"

As if to prove it, Fetch turned to Sally and took a great BIG sniff.

But all he could smell was …
BISCUITS.

THE END

SQUEAK!

PHILIP ARDAGH has won lots of awards, mostly for writing. Not one is for detecting. He's never had a dog, but if he did, he'd want one just like Fetch. Philip does have a big bushy beard, though, and they go everywhere together.

ELISSA ELWICK writes as well as illustrates, but, like Philip, never quite got the knack of detecting. She grew up with dogs around the house and hopes to have a real-life Fetch of her own one day. (She already has the bicycle and the basket.)